Contents

Written by Lisa Regan
Illustrated by Angelika Scudamore

First published 2016 by Brown Watson
The Old Mill, 76 Fleckney Road
Kibworth Beauchamp
Leicestershire LE8 0HG

ISBN: 978 0 7097 2307 3
© 2016 Brown Watson, England
Reprinted 2016, 2018
Printed in Malaysia

Now I Can

READ

Goodnight Stories

Brown Watson

ENGLAND

A Dirty Trick

Max and Minnie were playing. They had found a waterhole to wallow in, and were splashing around in the shallow water at the edge. Minnie used her trunk to scoop up some mud and throw it at Max.

SPLAT! The mud sailed through the air and landed on Max's forehead. He laughed and picked up an even bigger dollop to throw in Minnie's direction.

Minnie saw the mud heading straight for her. She ducked down out of the way. The mud flew over her head, and hit Great Aunt Gladys right between the eyes. Uh-oh!

Great Aunt Gladys trumpeted loudly. She was NOT happy! She wiped the mud from her face and thundered towards the water. What were Max and Minnie going to do? Minnie thought quickly...

She ran into the water, pushing Max ahead of her. Great Aunt Gladys did not want to follow them. Deeper and deeper they went. Soon they were totally covered, and poked their trunks out of the water so they could breathe.

They waited until they hoped the coast was clear. When they peeped above the water, they could see Great Aunt Gladys lumbering off into the distance. Phew! They were nice and clean again, too!

Read these words again

bigger

loudly

water

waited

sailed

laughed

landed

wallow

quickly

coast

breathe

distance

forehead

direction

What can you see here?

leaves

fishes

mud

elephant

waterfall

flowers

Caught in the Act

Bot was a robot. He lived in the bedroom of a little boy called Kieran. But Bot was a naughty toy, who liked to cause mischief in the night time.

He mixed up all the DVDs so they were in the wrong cases. He took the batteries out of the dinosaur so its eyes wouldn't flash. He turned up the volume on the electric organ so it was really loud.

Now, Kieran was a clever boy and he thought he knew who was to blame. One night, he curled up under his covers and pretended to be asleep. Really, he was awake, and watching.

He heard a whizz and a buzz as Bot whirred into action. Kieran peeped out from his bed and saw the cheeky robot heading for the jigsaw that lay, nearly finished, on the floor.

As quick as a flash, Kieran flicked a switch on a remote controller. His toy crane rolled across to where the robot stood, just about to steal a vital piece of the puzzle.

The robot bleeped as the crane swung down and scooped him up. 'Got you!' laughed Kieran, and he swung the crane around and left the robot in midair. And that's where he hangs every night, to keep him out of mischief!

Read these words again

quick   under

remote   awake

asleep   bedroom

laughed   mischief

action   naughty

cheeky   dinosaur

jigsaw   electric

What can you see here?

window

ball

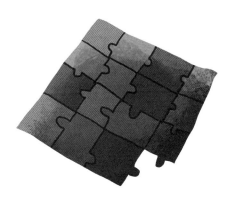

jigsaw puzzle

dinosaur

bed

books

How to Make an Ogre Happy

Once upon a time, there was an ogre. He lived in the biggest house in the village, with an enormous garden. All the children wanted to play there, but he was too grumpy to let them.

One day, a little boy kicked his football over the ogre's garden wall. The ogre saw it and roared, and kicked it straight back over the other side. He didn't want to play ball.

A little girl was sitting nearby, reading. A sudden gust of wind snatched up her comic, and blew it directly towards the ogre's garden. Oh no! What should she do? Timidly, she rang the doorbell.

The ogre answered the door and growled at her. In his hands were the shredded pages of the comic. He stuffed one page into his mouth, chewed it, and slammed the door. The little girl burst into tears.

Two little boys were walking past the ogre's garden, practising their tunes for the concert. As they reached his garden wall, they grew quiet so they wouldn't make the ogre angry.

The ogre wasn't roaring or growling, but he was whistling. Nervously, they played their tune again. The ogre whistled in time. Now, he always attends the village concerts, and sometimes even sings along. He loves music!

Read these words again

gust

garden

kicked

concert

roared

directly

village

slammed

chewed

whistling

nervously

quiet

straight

enormous

What can you see here?

audience

ball

cat

maracas

singer

ogre

Learning to Fly

Buster was nervous. It was his very first flying lesson today and he felt scared. His propeller wobbled and he thought he might cry. But Madame Roland, the flying instructor, took him under her wing.

'We will start gently,' she explained. 'Just a short trip, up into the sky and back down again. There is nothing to be afraid of. Just follow me and do what I do.'

Madame Roland trundled down the runway. Buster followed, watching very carefully. As they left the ground, Buster felt his heart do a loop the loop, but he lifted his wheels and stuck close behind her.

Wow! They were so high in the sky! Buster felt the wind rushing past, and couldn't take the smile off his face. Flying was amazing! He dipped one wing and wobbled slightly, then corrected himself.

Suddenly, Buster felt cold and wet. He couldn't see a thing, and he started to panic. Then he heard the reassuring rumble of Madame Roland's engines. 'Don't worry!' she shouted. 'It's only a cloud!'

Sure enough, they flew out and into clear blue skies once more. Buster grinned and speeded up. As he approached the next cloud, he knew what to expect. 'WHEEEEE!' he shouted. 'I am FLYING!'

Read these words again

follow

again

ground

behind

enough

panic

speeded

expect

nervous

flying

amazing

slightly

engines

carefully

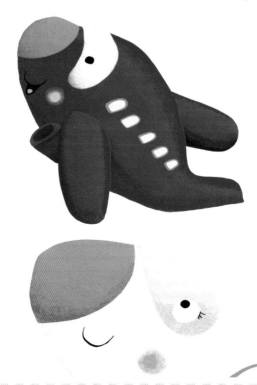

What can you see here?

flag

aeroplane

rainbow

control tower

buildings

runway

Play Time

Susie Saurus wanted to play. But no one would play with her. 'Please will you play hide and seek?' she asked. But her neck reached so high that she could easily see where all of her friends were hiding.

She asked Trudi Triceratops if she could join in her skipping game. But Susie's tail was so enormous that they couldn't find a skipping rope long enough. She got tangled all the time.

Victor Velociraptor was
playing ball with Vanya.
'Can I play, too?' asked Susie.
But she was so tall that she
grabbed the ball every time.
The others got bored and
wandered off.

Susie found Izzy Iguanodon
playing hopscotch by herself.
'Ooh, do you want some
company?' she asked. Izzy was
happy to have a friend – except
that Susie couldn't fit her big feet
inside the lines.

Hector Hadrosaur was building a den. 'I'll help!' said Susie. 'I can carry heavy branches, and pile them high!' But Susie's thunderous footsteps shook the ground, and knocked down the den every time.

Susie lay down and began to cry. Then Gabby Gallimimus and her family appeared. They jumped on Susie's back and slid down her tail. 'Hurray!' they squealed. 'You do make a good slide, Susie!'

Read these words again

began	skipping
wanted	appeared
jumped	company
heavy	except
ground	reached
hiding	would
inside	enormous

What can you see here?

flower

red dinosaur

leaves

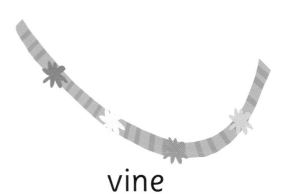

vine

foliage

skipping rope

A Helping Hand

'5-4-3-2-1...blast off!' shouted
Bradley, as his rocket engines
fired and launched him into space.
He looked out of the window as he
climbed higher, leaving Earth
far behind.

Bradley poured a glass of milk,
and settled down to watch a movie.
It was going to be a long trip.
Then he felt a judder, and a wobble,
and heard odd noises coming from
the engine room. Hmmm...

He would have to do an emergency landing. Bradley checked his space map to see if there was a planet anywhere near. He spotted a large, red planet with a big ! in the middle of it.

'Does that mean it isn't safe?' Bradley wondered. But he had no choice — nowhere else was close enough, and he had to fix his engine problems. He steered the rocket towards the planet.

He peeped out of the window nervously. Would the aliens here be big and scary, with sharp teeth or tentacles full of suckers? Would they gobble him up before he even had chance to ask for help?

Bradley crossed his fingers and hoped for the best. Luckily, the aliens here didn't have tentacles. Instead, they had hands like tools, so they could easily mend his engine. Thank goodness for that!

Read these words again

glass   planet
hoped   towards
scary   instead
engine   noises
red   poured
easily   climbed
choice   tentacles

What can you see here?

pink alien

planet

map

dog

purple alien

rocket

The Tooth Pixie

Poppy hated cleaning her teeth. It was so BORING! Each night, she would turn on the tap, squirt toothpaste down the plughole, and then run out of the bathroom. Her teeth were never clean.

One night, as Poppy turned off the tap, she heard a voice. 'Do it properly!' Poppy stared in surprise at a little man, perched on the side of the bathtub. 'I think you need my help!' said the man.

The little man had pointy ears and gleaming white teeth. He jumped up onto Poppy's shoulder and whispered in her ear. 'If you don't clean your teeth, I will steal all your biscuits!' he said.

Poppy didn't believe him. She laughed, and did her usual trick of pretending to clean her teeth. Then she rushed into her bedroom and hid under the covers.

The next day, Poppy's dad handed over her lunchbox. 'No biscuits today,' he said. 'There are none left in the cupboard. I don't know how we've run out so quickly.'

That night, Poppy brushed her teeth for two minutes, until they were sparkling clean. The little man nodded in approval. 'Very good,' he chuckled. 'But I'll be watching you! You can't hide from the Tooth Pixie!'

Read these words again

night

plughole

bathroom

clean

voice

properly

believe

shoulder

biscuits

pretending

usual

cupboard

quickly

watching

What can you see here?

lamp

teddy

pixie

mirror

duck

toothbrushes

Maddie's Lucky Day

Maddie and her mummy were going to visit Grandma. As they walked down the road, Maddie noticed something shiny on the pavement. 'Ooh, a penny!' said her mummy. 'That will bring you good luck.'

Maddie picked up the penny and skipped ahead. Suddenly, a black cat ran in front of her, and Maddie yelped in surprise. 'Don't worry,' said Mummy. 'Black cats are meant to bring good luck as well!'

Mummy held Maddie's hand as they crossed the road to the fields near Grandma's house. Two magpies were chattering on the fence. Mummy laughed. 'Some people think that's a lucky sign, too!'

Maddie smiled. She liked lucky days. She kicked through the long grass and poked the pretty flowers with her shoe. Mummy told her that they were clover flowers, and bees loved them.

'And guess what?' said Mummy. 'If you find a four-leafed clover...' Maddie knew the answer already. 'It will bring good luck!' she laughed, and started searching.

When Grandma opened the door, Maddie handed her a four-leafed clover and told her all their lucky signs. 'Well,' said Grandma. 'It is your lucky day – and I've baked your favourite cupcakes, too!'

Read these words again

baked

shiny

flowers

skipped

ahead

surprise

walked

noticed

pavement

crossed

field

searching

knew

guess

What can you see here?

hanging basket

butterflies

grandma

plant

cat

lady

Making Magic

Alfonso was practising his latest spell. He was trying to turn his toy soldier into a real life soldier who could run and climb and keep guard in his bedroom.
It wasn't going very well.

Every time Alfonso said the magic words, a puff of dirty green smoke appeared, and the soldier fell over. Alfonso sighed and propped him up again, and recited the spell one more time.

The spell still didn't work, so Alfonso laid his wand next to the soldier, and went down for his supper. When he came back upstairs, he stopped outside his bedroom door. He could hear strange noises.

He peeped around the door and gasped. All of his toy soldiers were marching in line! They paraded up and over his drawers, along his windowsill, and across his bed. Alfonso was amazed.

Alfonso crept into his room.
His marching soldiers were great fun,
but he needed to make them stop.
He waved his wand and muttered
some words. A puff of blue smoke
came out and his cars all zoomed
across the floor.

Help! This was all going wrong.
Alfonso took a deep breath. He
read his spell very carefully and
pronounced each word loudly. He
waved his wand...and silence fell on
his room. Phew!

Read these words again

magic	silence
smoke	loudly
dirty	sighed
supper	bedroom
upstairs	guard
wrong	soldier
drawers	paraded

What can you see here?

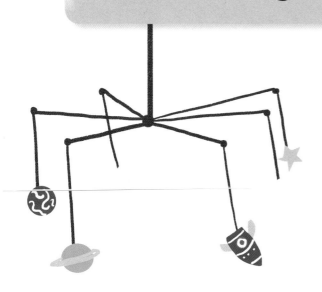

space mobile

toy cars

sock

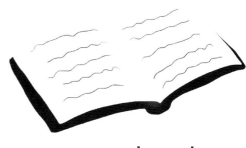

magic book

shelves

soldier

77

To the Rescue!

Rory was a firefighter. He went to work in a bright red fire truck. He loved putting out fires and helping in emergencies. His favourite thing was rescuing people from very tall buildings.

Rory's fire truck had a long ladder that extended up and up, high into the air. Rory would race up to the top with his hosepipe and squirt strong jets of water everywhere.

Rory worked with a firefighter called Cassie. Today, they were doing a fire drill. They drove to the park in the middle of town. Rory parked beneath the old oak tree, while Cassie opened up the ladder until it reached the top.

The children cheered as Cassie climbed up each rung of the ladder. They loved to watch the fire officers practise all of their safety operations. Rory kept watch below to make sure that Cassie was safe.

As Cassie reached the highest point of the ladder, she shouted down to Rory. 'I've found something!' She carefully leaned forward and picked a small helicopter out of the oak branches.

'It's my toy!' gasped Millie, down on the ground. 'It flew there last week and got stuck! Ooh, please can you rescue it for me?' Rory and Cassie smiled. Even fire drills have happy endings!

Read these words again

bright

water

please

forward

ladder

ground

branches

endings

rescue

safety

highest

beneath

helicopter

buildings

What can you see here?

helmet

hose

swings

roundabout

fire engine

flames

Time for Tea

Jake was very excited. His friend Cameron was playing at his house. Jake had a big secret to share with him. He ran to the bottom of the garden and proudly showed off the entrance to a small tunnel.

Jake got down on his knees and began to crawl inside. 'Follow me!' he shouted to Cameron. 'It is the best thing EVER – better than you could even think of in your best ever dreams!'

Cameron followed Jake down the tunnel. As they neared the end, the light grew bright and they could hear music. They crawled out, and straight into a circus. 'Is this real?' asked Cameron.

'It's magic!' explained Jake. 'Every time I crawl through, it is a different place at the end. Last week, it was Donut Land, and the time before that it was Pyjama Land, where you never have to get dressed!'

The two boys stayed at the circus for a long time. They laughed at the clowns, and gasped at the acrobats flying through the air. Then Jake said they really should go home.

Cameron asked if he could visit again soon. He loved the magic tunnel! And the next time they crawled along it together, they landed straight in Tea Party Land. That was a big hit, as you can imagine!

Read these words again

magic	showed
secret	crawled
music	imagine
friend	bright
shouted	laughed
dreams	straight
tunnel	pyjama

What can you see here?

cookies

drink

ice cream

popcorn

cake

sandwiches